A LIFE OF STARS LIBRARY®

VAT number 03624001206

LIFE OF   STARS

PARADOXICAL DANCE

VIKTOR A. KING

ENGLISH VERSION

CHAPTER ONE

Hayden Planetarium – New York City

Date: December 24, 2023

Time: 6:47 PM

Susy decided to organize the final documents before closing the office.

It was Christmas Eve.

She sighed.

It was Christmas Eve for many – a tree adorned with lights and ribbons, gifts, and terracotta figurines emulating centuries of history.

Friends and family gratifying the ego with hugs and tenderness.

She adjusted her high-necked sweater; the wool pinched her skin, and she scratched the whiteness of her neck with bitten nails, causing an immediate reddish spot.

She wore a ponytail, with a few unruly strands and a perfect fringe reminiscent of an eternal child.

A round turtle-shell frame emphasized the congenital myopia she had suffered from since her early school days.

Overall, she was a pleasant woman – not beautiful, certainly not flashy, but pleasant.

The kind of woman you notice when drunk or depressed, invariably lingering in the corners of a room, in the deserted armchairs. A woman who had enjoyed little, with an unrelenting inner voice always suggesting her to stop. Stop at the pedestrian crossings, at the red traffic light, stop at the tram station, stop in front of life experiences because thinking about them or enduring the consequences, even if pleasant, was too exhausting.

Especially if pleasant.

The real terror for a woman like her was not anonymity or the boring routine of a life without risks, preordained in every detail, but happiness.

How do you endure happiness? It is genuinely challenging to face a real, indisputable, spasmodic dose of joy. An excess of endorphins, a galloping endocrine dose of irrational oxytocin flooding the body, providing satisfaction, pride, confidence.

Better the flat control of a utility vehicle, a few trotting horses, a gentle clutch, a reliable brake, a subdued accelerator.

She had no love life, was not inclined to flirt, not inclined to undress or be touched, so few courted her, having to navigate through shirt buttons, collars too high and inaccessible, jeans, sneakers, and woolen socks.

No one at Christmas would have asked her for an obscene pose or to spread her legs in a gift stream. She would be awaited by the cat, two multicolored parakeets defying old age, and a reheated dinner. Her Christmas tree was the ugliest in the world – few lights, ornaments accumulated over centuries, dust settled on almost dry branches.

She took off her glasses, cleaned the lenses with the suede of the case, two slight scratches caused a hint of annoyance. She saw the world blurred with an unnecessary outline of two transversal lines.

Her job was monotonous; she read mail, forwarded emails, and made sure there were no complaints about access to the Planetarium. Occasionally, she forwarded press releases and organized sporadic visits with New York schools. She was inclined towards negligence, in her body, relationships, and work. But it seemed her presence was essential, so she wisely ensured money every month for rent, food, and some clothing from the department stores. New York was an unbearable city to live in – too much crime, too big, divided, multicultural, dirty, and with a perpetually sweet smell like fast-food barbecue sauce.

A huge city entirely enclosed in a smart experience. Smart was the time to breathe it and visit it before enclosing yourself in a protected environment, home, and work.

She shut down the computer, took the keys to lock the last doors, and turned off the lights in the most important rooms. About ten minutes remained until the end of her shift. It didn't matter if she was punctual; she had nothing planned afterward, but she didn't feel like coming home late. Perhaps someone would set off fireworks, and her cat could get scared.

She opened the last letter. On plain paper, without a sender's address, rather anonymous, typed in Times New Roman 12 on the computer. The sheet was white, perfectly centered, with eleven lines in bold:

"In the darkness of the night, under the starry sky, resides an enigma, dreamt by many.

No beginning, no end, without time or space. Among numbers and secrets, it hides its palace. An enchanted glass sphere in an unknown world. Keys and locks, everything is guarded here.

Stars are guides, but the path is dark.

Decipher the code, reveal its future."

She couldn't stand rhymes, didn't understand them, didn't understand why waste time reflecting on the meaning of something when you could simply write the answer!

She couldn't decipher anything, and consequently, she was not interested in unveiling her future. She crumpled the letter and tossed it into the waste bin with the scraps.

She stood up, grabbed her wool coat and hat, and headed to turn off the remaining lights. Christmas was really nonsense, devoid of magic for adults accustomed to the monotony of reality!

She entered the corridor leading to the large hall, the one that usually hosted groups, screens with ovalized lenses covering the entire oval wall, amplifying the majestic view of the sky.

The corridor was sterile, illuminated by neon lights along almost a meter of its perimeter. On the floor, constellations were drawn that lit up in the dark when the lights were turned off in the evening – an incredible spectacle, like walking through the Universe.

On the walls, paintings and testimonies of millennia of human work in search of the meaning of life beyond Earth.

"Susssyyy... Susssyyy...."

She heard a whisper in the dim light, hissing yet childlike, like a child playing hide and seek.

"Who's there? I can't see you..."

"I'm here!" a figure emerged from the wall. A childlike figure, iridescent, resembling a nine-year-old girl with long blonde tails, an angelic robe, and golden cords tied to the ends and long almost-white hair.

She had big blue eyes and a mouth shaped like a rose, a carmine red almost jarring with the ethereal beauty of her robes.

"What are you doing here?" Susy wasn't frightened; it was normal for a child to get lost. Usually, they called the police and entrusted the child to them until the parents came to pick them up.

"I'm here for you..."

Susy was surprised and widened her pupils.

"For me? Why on earth? I don't think I know you..."

"I am your future self, what you will become, unfortunately now..."

She spread her little arms, and behind her, two large swan wings unfolded to the edges of the corridor.

Susy stepped back.

She even seemed larger and more majestic than when she first appeared.

"Is this a joke?" she chirped in a shrill voice.

"No, I can't help you now. I tried throughout your life; I gave you several chances not to be here tonight, yet you ignored them, and now here you are, and he will arrive now. I just wanted to tell you that it will be very fast, and after that, you will be with me. Don't be afraid; you won't be alone anymore because where you're going, there will be many like you."

She reached out and gently caressed Susy's cheek. Then, she dissolved.

She gradually became transparent until she disappeared exactly as silently as she had arrived.

Susy was stunned. She couldn't imagine that anyone could concoct such a prank, a stupid prank.

She stopped in the corridor, touching the wall and supporting herself breathlessly.

"What a stupid prank..." she whispered. The lights suddenly went out. Susy screamed. Darkness enveloped her. She fumbled to lean against the wall. "Remember, Susy, relax, breathe, memorize the corridor, twenty steps, and you're in the large hall..." she encouraged herself and took the first step. The heat in the corridor increased; it felt like tropical warmth, the fans must have broken, right now, that's why the lights went out. Images from the latest news came to her mind – "BEATEN TO DEATH ON THE APARTMENT BALCONY, WIFE TORTURED BY HUSBAND, STABBED AND LOCKED IN THE TRUNK OF HER CAR, BABY PROSTITUTES RAPED AND STRANGLED..." These terrible things happened; the news told her about them every day. The heat and darkness were stifling. "Is anyone there? Can anyone hear me?" "I hear you!" a loud laughter tore through the air. "Who is it? Where are you? I can't see you!" "Where I am, it's dark... it's the lights of Eternity, and it's very, very hot!" another laughter invaded the corridor, seeming to come from every corner and nowhere, metallic and rough, thick and bestial. "Where are you? Show yourself!" The light of a match appeared near Susy.

The shadow behind the match was that of a wild boar with glowing eyes and ibex horns, fur on its neck and chest.

"What is happening? Who are you? What kind of prank is this?"

"I am your executioner," it proclaimed tonelessly.

"Exe... executioner? What are you talking about?" Susy swallowed to control herself. Fear surged from her stomach with a rush of sour bile. Her legs trembled; she felt them weak and eager to give in. She remembered the Popeye cartoon; it always made her laugh that the characters, when scared, started trembling right from their knees. So, it was true, it happened like that.

"I won't be the hand, but I am the mind that created it! Have you solved the riddle?"

"Riddle?" she whispered, the saliva disappeared from her mouth.

"Shall I repeat it? Want me to? Let's see if you can do it... if you can, maybe we'll have more fun!"

"In the darkness of the night, under the starry sky, resides an enigma, dreamt by many. No beginning, no end, without time or space. Among numbers and secrets, it hides its palace. An enchanted glass sphere in an unknown world. Keys and locks, everything is guarded here. Stars are guides, but the path is dark. Decipher the code, reveal its future."

"I don't know... I don't understand... let me go..." Susy whimpered.

"What a sad life you've led! No one will mourn you! You have no relatives, friends; you don't have a man or woman to lie with and procreate. You haven't built anything! You've gorged on ice cream and sweets only to vomit them out, scared by the kilos expanding your belly! You haven't had children; you've never given anything! And you will receive nothing! No one will look for you... they will discover your rotting corpse after the holidays and wonder why your disappearance wasn't reported! Do you have any idea of the solution?"

"No, I... no."

"Angels lie, you know... more than me! It's not true that you'll end up with them because when all of this is over, grrrr He will realize that you are useless and hand you over to me..."

The match went out.

Darkness enveloped her again.

Susy screamed.

A rustle moved away from her.

Her heart pounded in her chest, almost deafening her ears.

She took a deep breath. Inhaled and exhaled slowly. Inhaled and exhaled again.

"Now I move forward! I'm not afraid!"

She just needed to reach the large hall, the central planetarium; the cosmic light would guide her to the light switch and the telephone to alert the night security.

She took a step and another, sliding her hands along the wall until she reached the corner with the door.

Her fingertips rejoiced. She directed them in step with her belly, and the panic bar handle.

She pushed.

She had done it! The door gave way, and she was inside the planetarium.

The chiaroscuro became sharper. The starlight was of a dense blue.

She headed towards the light panel.

A ticking joined the sound of her own steps.

It sounded like a metronome.

Piano notes filled the space between Susy and the light panel.

A timid drop of sweat crossed her forehead.

It seemed like Chopin's Prelude.

Not that she understood piano music, but a memory, perhaps a lesson from a childhood friend, suggested the nature of those notes.

Nature? There are no pianos here... yet acoustically, they seemed like keyboard notes. Like an old piano with wooden keys and chords in the case.

She froze in place.

Footsteps overlapped the metronome.

And they were coming towards her.

She was motionless, liquefied.

Her legs didn't respond to her command; she should have turned. She should have quickened her pace and reached the light panel. Yet, like night cats on the streets, she immobilized herself.

Her ears became sensitive receptors. Like facing a blinding light, the darkness paralyzed her.

The footsteps approached. She heard a labored, panting breath.

She felt compassion for herself.

She turned slowly. She knew from movies that seeing would make her destiny real.

Two eyes stared at her, much taller than hers. The rest was black, maybe a hood?

A hand rose above their heads and collapsed onto her head.

The black became darker.

She fell.

Fainted.

Was she dead? Already?

Two hands took her neck, squeezed until she lost consciousness. They had white silk gloves. And long hands.

A slight pressure on the carotid artery was enough; the air didn't filter, creating a slight muscular ataxia and loss of consciousness.

She was lifted, limbs bound with stars, and the last cord around her neck, then swayed like a swing. Her bones creaked, making sinister sounds. The neck vertebrae detached first, ligaments resisted, stretching until the inevitable. Arms separated from shoulders, thighs from hips, the head from the neck, yet the entire body remained intact, held by flesh and skin. Until the swaying ceased, and like Christ to the notes of Chopin, Susy hung beneath the celestial dome

CHAPTER TWO

NYPD 24th Precinct

Date: December 25, 2023

Time: 1:13 AM

Adam rested the device with immense sadness. The hurried voices of the corridors abducted him for a moment. A prostitute was complaining about the treatment.

"Detective! Detective!"

"Yes, James, I heard, let's go."

The patrol car was ready in the parking lot; the planetarium was in their district, impossible to skip duty. He hoped to finish the shift in peace, go to his apartment, and rest in silence. It was Christmas, for Christ's sake!

"Detective? Adam? Everything okay?"

"Yes, James, relax, I'm here! At this hour, without traffic, we'll be there in about ten minutes. I'll use the siren, not that we need it, but you never know. At Christmas, it seems like the law works the other way around, more villains instead of more good guys! The Sergeant informed me it's a mess, prepare yourself... the end-of-year maniac..."

He smiled tightly; wrinkles on the sides of his eyes framed a tough, angular face, vaguely angular, like Van Gogh's paintings. Blond hair kept long behind the ears and a hint of a beard on the gaunt cheeks softened the sharp features.

Adam had been a detective for too little time to earn the privilege of peace at Christmas and too long to relax during the holidays. He knew that evil was nestled in every mind, even the most unlikely. Nestled and ready to reveal itself in its magnificence. Because evil had something magnificent, from "facio," Latin. Facio facis, to do, evil did, he thought, operated. It produced various actions, one following the other, to manifest itself, from "manifesto," glorifying its work.

Here was evil once again manifest, at the NY Planetarium. They entered, overcoming the barriers already orchestrated to keep the public and the curious away.

"The forensic team?" he asked the first cop, a kid just over eighteen, red-faced and red-haired with what could be a constellation of freckles on his entire beardless face.

"They're already on-site, I'll take you, Detective. You'll see what a show; they haven't brought her down yet... they waited for you..." he sniffed.

"Impressive, isn't it?"

He whispered, "Honestly, yes, I'm sorry for her..."

"Don't feel pity, officer! Or you won't be able to defend yourself when necessary. You'll think with your conscience, not with the instinct for self-preservation."

He fell silent.

The scene that appeared to Adam was gothic and surreal. A girl hanging in the center of the planetarium dome, suspended by ropes tied with boat knots, with limbs too long to respect the symmetry of the body, evidently disjointed from the trunk, including the breast, supported by the fifth rope but hanging with all the hair at an irregular 90° angle too irregular to be registered as normal by the human eye. A ponytail hung down her body, woolen clothes, long pants, sneakers, one fallen to the ground, probably lost while they hoisted her.

"Bring her down, for God's sake!"

"Adam..." approached James, the district sergeant, calmly resumed speaking.

"No signs of struggle, post-mortem bruising, she was probably still alive but unconscious when they hoisted and anchored her, the neck went first, then the rest of the limbs."

"Let's look around, photos aren't enough for me, we'll review the autopsy report later."

"The keys fell here, near the light panel, where the first struggle probably took place." James pointed to the abandoned keys on the ground.

Adam bent down, supporting himself on the tips of his toes, with his hands clasped between his knees and flat stomach.

"There are two blood drops here, likely from the victim, but have them examined. They are about twenty centimeters away from the keys. I think they're a mix of saliva and gingival blood, due to a blow to the face that made her lose consciousness and drop the keys. The assailant was evidently taller; the drops are diagonal with a narrow angle of about 25°, meaning the blow came from above to reach the neck, cheek at least another twenty centimeters away. The victim is normally 1 meter and sixty, so the murderer is between 1 meter and eighty to 1 meter and ninety in height."

Adam stared at where the assailant might have appeared, where he could have hidden, waiting for her.

"Let's summarize, James, it's crucial. She's heading for the panel, why is it dark? The murderer turned off the lights, so he was waiting for her. He knew she would go there, and he approaches her from behind, where is he hiding, after turning off the power?"

Adam scanned the crime scene in a quick overview.

"It seems apparently clear of hiding spots, the large central observatory, planets hanging to recreate the galaxy, some scattered displays, but otherwise an open space. He wasn't afraid of being discovered. He knew he would surprise the victim. And that she wouldn't withstand physical confrontation. Indeed, she's not wearing protective gear, right?"

"She was an employee, a normal employee, without a family. I checked her desk, no photos or clues that she had a full private life. And from how she's dressed and her build, she seems fragile," replied the sergeant regretfully.

"Where did she enter from?" Adam asked breathlessly.

"Through the main door, a long corridor connects the hall to the offices. The panic handle has her prints and was completely open. So, she must have exerted all her strength, perhaps already running away..."

"It's possible. Let's look, take me there."

James stepped back and turned towards the wide-open door.

"True, I think you're right. If she had to come in to turn off the lights normally, she would have also closed it. Instead, she arrived with the lights off; she forced it open, knowing that the solution was inside, namely the light panel. She came from the corridor; maybe she was already scared. Now we need to figure out if there's another panel, and which one is closer. Because if that's the case, then the lights went out when she was approaching the hall, and she was forced to go where they attacked her."

Adam retraced the corridor; some paintings caught his attention, two close together in the middle of the corridor were askew.

"She leaned here. Here is where the light went out."

"Yes, true, Adam. Let's check the desk again. Better."

Adam opened the office, pushing the door aside with a pen and entering along the walls.

"First, let's inspect the whole place. Then, the desk. Please take notes."

"Okay."

"Desk clear, a PC – check the password, a stack of well-organized papers. An orderly victim. No photos, no trinkets. A comfortable chair, she must have had back pain. The trash can, there are some papers, let's have a look. Receipts, district letters, Mayor's letters, advertisements, and a sheet, at the bottom, crumpled. The others torn. Why at the bottom, why did she discard it differently? We open it with gloves; it could be evidence."

Adam put on rubber gloves.

He read aloud.

"In the darkness of the night, under the starry sky, resides an enigma, dreamt by many. Without a beginning, nor an end, without time or space. Among numbers and secrets, it conceals its palace. Enchanted glass sphere, in an unknown world. Keys and locks, everything is guarded here. Stars are guides, but the path is obscure. Decode the code, unveil your future."

"What does it mean?" James asked.

"It's the planetarium, the key to his future is the planetarium, so it's an invitation to go into the room. The murderer wrote it, A4 paper, light watermark, Times New Roman font, printed with black ink, have the ink analyzed. But why at the bottom of the trash can? The paper and ink will be normal, any A4 printer with a universal cartridge, certainly, but why at the bottom... he must have received it tonight, must have read it before dying. Why at the bottom of the trash can then?"

"The murderer was here, afterward!" James almost shouted.

"Yes, I think so... he was looking for the letter, overturned the trash can, wanted to make sure it was there or that she had read it, but by then she was dead... so it's for us. To make us understand that he is a serial killer and has a key to kill."

"Damn, Christmas couldn't have been worse..."

"See, there's some dirt here, on the floor, he overturned the trash can, there's the tempered graphite of the pencils, then put everything back in place. Have fingerprints taken here too... we won't find anything, he certainly had gloves. The painting, is there another one?"

Adam looked around, heading towards various switches on the wall in front, with colored labels under each switch.

"Here it is, in his office... it's clear that she turned off everything with the light, then died halfway down the hallway. The murderer was here to take her away. Where did he come in from?"

"From anywhere... The observatory is open to the public, they were closing, at six they had let out the last visitors, she had stayed to close the offices and the rest."

"Yes, true... a dead end."

"Shall we go to the Central?"

"I would like to see the rigor mortis; you know that the last images are imprinted on the pupil? And she saw the murderer..." Adam scratched his beard; it had been itching since he decided to let it grow.

"She was hanging between the Sun and Mercury. She was the first."

James looked thoughtful: "It could be, but also a coincidence...."

"There are no coincidences with a serial killer, I believe he left other clues that we haven't found yet."

"Do you want to check the body? Stop the forensic team; they're taking it to the autopsy."

"Yes, thank you... I'm perplexed... what sense does it make for him or her, the victim? Did they really choose anyone at random? Why leave her an enigma to solve? They knew her... Or at least, the victim was part of a pattern, a pawn."

Adam walked down the corridor; the corpse had been placed inside a body bag. An assistant opened the zipper and revealed the face and chest.

The eyes were wide open, the pupils dilated.

"Photograph the pupil."

She wasn't ugly, just anonymous.

Adam pushed aside the wool sweater; underneath, she wore plain white cotton underwear from a department store. The undershirt neatly tucked into the edges of the panties.

The pants were fastened.

"There's no violence, no struggle, obvious. Check the nails...."

James intervened: "Her name was Susan Bloom, no parents but a sister, lives here in NY, Eve Bloom, let me get the address, and we'll go, okay detective?"

"Yes, okay, excellent." He scratched his beard again, an anonymous girl with a sister in the same city.

"Is the sister older or younger?"

"Younger, she's divorced, no kids, no fines, works as a saleswoman inside The Shops at Columbus Circle in Central Park, rents in Central Park, bank accounts okay, health insurance okay, she's healthy, thirty-seven years old."

"Okay, James, well done. Let's go up; we still have to give her the news anyway."

CHAPTER THREE

5736 Central Park West, PH 15°

Date: December 25, 2023

Time: 3:04 AM

Adam adjusted the collar of his beige raincoat; he never wore a tie and shirt but rather a light cashmere V-neck sweater and a white T-shirt. He didn't like formalities; Nike and jeans were definitely more comfortable and suitable if he had to chase a criminal.

Certainly, the Detective's job didn't imply chasing someone but thinking, observing, and thinking again to draw profitable conclusions. That was ultimately his job. Although equipped with a Glock 19 9mm semi-automatic pistol, undoubtedly infallible, as demonstrated by his recent training at the police firing range. It was there, cold and silent, lying in the holster strapped to his back, next to his left rib.

With a chambered round, always.

It wasn't necessary to cock the processor to shoot, only to draw it and take aim. It was the NYPD Agency's policy that wanted its men secure on the streets.

The most difficult task was communicating death news to relatives. He could clearly sense when they were relieved or saddened, and often relief prevailed. We were inhumane in this century, too selfishly absorbed in our square of rotten land to be sorry for someone's death, especially a relative who either brought inheritance or relieved inconvenience with their accidental departure.

It was unpleasant to notice the slight curling of lips; they didn't even realize it, but their thoughts manifested in their bodies—a glint in the eyes, fleeting, cheeks reddening, hands joining in a prayer of thanks... thanks that you eliminated the maniac uncle, the cheating wife, the drug-addicted son, thank you, thank you, God, for taking away a problem without me doing anything, comfortably asleep in my bed.

But, that time, the time when he rang Eve Bloom's doorbell, he knew he would encounter genuine regret. This clear and decisive perception vividly emerged from his left rib, the one trying to warm the Glock 19.

He imagined her eyes would moisten, that her voice would be broken, and a slight trembling in her hands. Why did he imagine this? Because of the brutality of the crime. We don't care about death, only about gruesome death because it could have happened to us, and in a sort of collective repentance, we regret it.

James diligently rang the doorbell.

We heard the shuffle of slippers and an anxious voice responding from behind the closed door.

"Who is it?" a female voice asked.

"New York Police, please open."

"Police? Show me your badge through the peephole." Smart...

I showed her the badge and badge number. We heard her unlocking the door, leaving only one secure and slightly ajar to look at her interlocutors. I still couldn't make out her features.

"What can I do for you? It's very late..."

"We know, please open; we need to report news that concerns you personally, and we can't do it from the landing," I replied courteously.

She sighed. "Alright, I'll open, wait a second, I'll put on a robe."

She closed the door. After a few minutes, she opened it, holding it with one hand or gripping it.

She knew.

She knew that bad news was coming; she had read it on our faces.

I found myself facing the most beautiful woman I had ever seen. Completely different from her sister, she was very blonde with long, fine, straight hair down to her waist, intensely green eyes with a particular cat-like shape, pronounced cheekbones, and a full, pronounced, and provocative mouth that clashed with the elegance of her petite and tall figure, except for the fact that it was absolutely and evidently natural. As if God wanted to give her a provocative mouth to make her exceed and everything else to elegantly refrain from life's negligences.

She was without makeup and wonderful, wearing a cream-colored silk robe, tied at the waist with pompom-pink pom-poms. With the long, ringless hand with well-groomed and polished nails in an elegant coral red, she closed the robe at neck level.

She stepped aside and let us in.

The environment was very refined. A stunning view of the city from the windows that dominated the entire room. A huge Roche Bobois Nuvola sofa dominated the center, lamps and paintings adorned the walls, a soft cream-colored wool carpet lay gently on the pink Carrara marble floor.

"Please, take a seat..." she whispered.

It was evident that she would wait for the news, like any well-mannered lady; she would hold back her emotions until the inevitable. But as long as we didn't get there, it was still permissible to hope it was something else.

"Are you Mrs. Eve Bloom?" James asked, not at all overwhelmed by the beauty of the woman in front of him.

"Miss..."

"Do you have a sister named Susan Bloom, who works as a clerk at the New York Planetarium?"

I noticed the surprise in her vivid green eyes. A subtle flash that slightly widened the pupil. She remained impassive for the rest.

"Yes, she works there, I lost contact with my sister since her marriage... What happened?"

"How long has it been since you last communicated with your sister?" James asked again.

She looked directly at me, deliberately seeking my eyes fixed on her face. She knew I outranked her.

"What happened?"

I couldn't lower my gaze; I wanted to escape, truly, I wanted to go back in time, to the time when I enlisted, to decide to be someone else, but not this person who had to tell her the truth. But she nailed me with her wonderful green eyes. Nailed me to the cream-colored Roche Bobois Nuvola model.

"Your sister is dead; she was killed tonight, a few hours ago," I told her in one breath.

She paled beyond the diaphanous pallor of her face, widened her eyes, and pressed her lips together to hold back the scream that evidently rose in her throat.

The hands, which were clasped in her lap, clawed at the robe, as if it were the handkerchief she didn't have, like the widows of nobles who, in grief, hid behind embroidered lace handkerchiefs.

"Dead?" she whispered lightly, with forces abandoning not only her face but also the body that bent in on itself, to hide from the evidence.

"Do you want a sip of water?" I asked dutifully.

I would have preferred to die rather than be remembered by her for that nefarious occasion.

She focused on me again, her eyes full of unexpressed tears. In that moment, I felt such irresistible compassion (love) for that unknown woman, holding back, shaken by surprise, that I only wanted to hug her and protect her.

I stood up and headed to the kitchen, took a crystal glass from the minimalist cupboard and filled it with fresh tap water. Then I offered it to her.

She refocused on me; a tear slid from her left eye. She didn't see me; I was evidently a blurry figure in front of her bewildered gaze.

James continued, "We're sorry for your pain, Miss Bloom, but we need to ask you some questions, are you ready?"

"Ready?" she whispered; her voice broke as if she had run a long uphill race only to discover that beneath her, there was nothing.

"We need to ask you if you knew if your sister had any obvious enemies, people who followed her or harassed her with messages or anything. If she had a boyfriend with whom she had ended things, or inconvenient lovers." James's tact annoyed me.

"Lovers? Boyfriend?" She shook her head; a few tears escaped, and she regained color.

She accepted the glass of water I offered, refocused on me.

"We hadn't spoken in three years and a few months..." she looked at her hands. The right one, the one over her heart, came to her aid and wiped away another escaped tear.

"Try to remember..." James insisted, was he immune to the charm of this woman?

"I don't remember her having any flings; she was very reserved... how did it happen?" and she turned her sorrowful gaze towards me.

I blushed like a child. I averted my gaze; I had been caught.

"Death is death, no matter how it happens. Could you know the passwords for her phone and computer?" I asked to recover, even in front of James, who was looking at me with a small mocking smile.

"I really don't know, maybe her birthdate or her name. I repeat, I haven't seen her in years, since... since I got married."

"What happened?" I asked out of curiosity; I wanted to know why such a beautiful woman was alone, if she was alone, but above all, to hear the sound of her voice, gentle.

"On the day of my wedding, she told me I would be unhappy, that my now ex-husband wouldn't make me happy, quite the opposite... we argued, I accused her of being a dry, faithless woman. She was right, but I never told her... I divorced after less than a year; he was cheating on me." She finished the story in one breath.

She swallowed some sadness and continued.

"I'm really shocked; I regret never having said anything nice to her, how beautiful and passionate she was about her work. I regret that our parents, in the end, blatantly preferred me over her, and that this preference filled me with pride, not regret. I've been really... terrible." Her voice broke, and she sobbed with her face in her hands, like the divas of the 1930s, like the beautiful women for whom every gesture is charm and attention, for whom every breath is an opportunity.

"We're leaving, Miss Bloom. I invite you to the station tomorrow at 12:00 PM; is that okay? We'll need to write a brief statement and try to understand. I hope you agree...?" I invited, praying that she would be cooperative and that she might also want to see me a little, even in horrible circumstances.

"You have to identify the body; you're the closest relative," James added.

She visibly twitched, then stood up straight between us.

"Absolutely not!"

She was elegant and beautiful; her small breasts rose in her defense, nipples like armed soldiers, small round, soft breasts. I stared at the neckline of the robe that had opened, revealing the hollow of her neck, the lace of the nightshirt, the whiteness of her soft skin. A brief erection seized me, and terribly embarrassed, I stepped back.

"James, let's go, not now, we'll talk about it tomorrow. And I headed to the door.

She followed us, evidently relieved that we were leaving.

James turned abruptly, addressing her, "What do you do, Miss? This apartment is very beautiful and expensive..."

She blushed; she had caught the insinuation.

"I'm the manager of the Dior flagship store, you know they pay me well, the apartment is a benefit..."

"Maybe some admirer that your sister had warned you about?" he insisted.

She shook her head, genuinely considering it.

"No, I don't think so. She didn't know what I was doing, and my life changed completely after the divorce. Yes, I have various admirers who lavish gifts on me, and she would have disapproved, but she didn't know. She was out of my life, so I don't see any reason to kill her. Are we sure it's murder?"

"Why do you ask?" I interrupted.

We were close and at the same height; her intoxicating vanilla scent vaguely stunned me.

"Because I thought she would have committed suicide if she had remained alone, and I believe she was alone. Are you sure they... that they..."

"Yes," I told her.

"It's very sad. Some people are born with a marked destiny, in a somewhat inevitable way. She was like that."

"Another question, Miss... Have you received any special letters recently? Puzzles? Rhymes?" I asked, suddenly afraid for her, as if a premonition of something we were facing together.

"This is a strange question... yes, I'm part of an intelligence club, one of those activities for the rich, a bit alternative... we solve puzzles, the smartest ones win beyond the glory of intellect, also benefits like trips, jewelry, and so on."

We listened to her in silence, but I knew James had understood.

"I think you are in serious danger. Show me some ways to compete in your intelligence club."

"It's not called that; it has a Greek name, Noetike Synaxis. We participate on Mondays from 6:00 PM for about two hours; the location is communicated with a rhyme and changes every time."

"How is it communicated?" I asked very seriously.

She got scared; it was evident that she believed me.

"With a... letter... why?" I grabbed her shoulders, shaking her slightly; her safety was at stake.

"Show them to me! How do the letters arrive? By mail?"

"Y-yes."

"Where are they?!"

"I throw them... I didn't know... the last one was last week; I have to wait for the next one... it arrives today!"

"This morning? It's impossible; mail doesn't arrive on Christmas! How do they deliver it to you?"

"Adam..." James was pulling my arm. I was overreacting.

Unfortunately, it was already personal.

"When there are holidays, I think they deliver them personally, but they arrive...

you'll see that tomorrow I'll have the summons." She shrugged and pointed to the door.

"Okay, tomorrow at noon at our place! And bring the letter. This is my phone number; call me for any suspicious noise." I handed her my business card, opened her right hand, and placed it on her palm. Then I shook it, enclosing it between mine.

She stared at me in fear, pale as death, with wide-open eyes of an incredibly intense and true green.

"Now take something relaxing, a tea, a glass of water, close the door properly, and go to bed," James added to end the visit with dignity.

"Thank you, I suppose."

And she closed the door behind us.

We distinctly heard the sound of the bolt.

Eve headed to the bathroom; the mirror reflected a ghost. She darkened.

Susy dead? OH MY GOD!

People could die young, even among acquaintances...

Yet, it had been so long since she had seen her; did she really feel sorry?

"Do you really feel sorry... remember you two as little girls in the garden, running innocent, no one had divided you yet, no one had insinuated evil into you..."

Behind her, a girl dressed in white, with long braids and a mischievous nose, stared at her.

"Do I have hallucinations? Who are you?"

"I'm a friend of yours and Susy's... now I'm here to help you..."

"Do you know Susy?"

"I tried to help her many times; I suggested she call you... a smile from a child, a note with your name... an unexpected coincidence, but she always wanted to pretend nothing was happening! It was too hard to overcome pride..."

"Are you her friend? How did you get in? With the police?"

"No, I'm here to help you, all of us want to; don't be afraid, we are good."

Large swan wings unfolded behind her, occupying the entire bathroom space.

"What... I... I can't believe it..."

"Yes, I know; it's better this way; I'm a dream, okay? You have to say okay."

"OK."

"Now don't worry; I'm leaving. You will remember it was a dream, okay?"

"OK."

"We want to help you; we care about you. We want you to be happy and loved. Remember Susy, remember that you loved her, she was your sister, help the police, and you'll see that you will be protected."

"OK."

"Please, it's time to go to sleep; you will have a long restorative sleep. The word

you're   missing   is   MilkyWay...
remember."

"Milky Way? What does it mean?"

And she disappeared.

Literally faded until she became
transparent and then vanished
completely, leaving the bathroom with
the porcelain bathtub, the shower, and
the two sinks.

CHAPTER FOUR

"She had to identify the body... it was the protocol!"

"Tomorrow, we'll go there now," Adam started the car; he was still evidently disturbed.

Office of Chief Medical Examiner – Manhattan

Date: 25 December, 2023

Time: 4:12 AM

They crossed the threshold of the Medical Examiner's office about twenty minutes later. The lights were dazzling.

"Hey, Smitty, everything okay? Still the nights..."

Smith Gerald Housband, medical examiner, divorced, two children to support, overweight with incipient baldness, and an IQ of 160.

"Hey there, Guys! How's it going? Terrible about the girl, huh? Susan... are you ready? Nothing significant in the stomach, no drugs, no food. Probably had a normal breakfast and then nothing for lunch. Carotid clear, even though broken, the cause of death. Nothing in the iris, the black part; technically, she died by hanging. No hair, fur, or foreign fibers compared to what she was wearing."

"Ouch, I was hoping for something..."

"I know, Adam, but now they've gotten clever. They wear gloves, clean the body. What can I say, it's a mess, for me."

"Come on, continue. Any signs of violence?"

"No, but there was a strange thing inserted into her vagina. This is where you'll go crazy!"

"In the vagina? But she had her jeans perfectly closed, and the undershirt inside her panties. Who does that? Someone without a boyfriend expecting a lonely night..."

"In fact, she wasn't shaved, neither thighs nor groin. She was, let's say, a bit unkempt. But it seems our little monster found it intriguing to put a little something inside her and seal the package well."

"What, Smitty?"

"A star! One of those glow-in-the-dark stars that you stick to the walls of rooms as decals. It's plastic, not adhesive, with five points, and it was shining like crazy inside the cervix."

"Where is it?"

"Voilà!" He handed us the specimen, placed on the microscope slide.

"About 0.5 mm, nothing much, easy to put in, but zero prints, nothing in the mucous membranes. I'm sorry, I checked."

"Is there a brand? Where are they sold?"

"But, Adam, it's Christmas! Everywhere!"

I scratched my forehead; my hair had grown too long. We stared at each other in silence for a moment.

"Any leads?"

"Zero, I'd say..."

Except for the fear that Eve Bloom might be involved as the next victim.

"What about the rope knots?"

"Tied by an experienced sailor, they would have held a buffalo! Zero prints, zero evidence, probably done with latex gloves, the sturdy kind, like surgeon's gloves."

"All we can do is wait for the letter tomorrow," I reluctantly admitted.

"Letter? Oh yes, I saw it, examined it. Normal paper, printed with universal ink. It could be anything, from anywhere."

"The neck and arms could have detached naturally, but the legs? Did they pull them?"

"The knots, the ropes were connected. The weight of the neck and arms tightened the other two, like sawed and portioned... an expert, or a killer who took a long time to prepare."

"Could it be a woman?" James asked, who had remained in silent contemplation until then.

"The possibility shouldn't be ruled out. The victim was very small, unprepared, so even a muscular woman could have had the upper hand. Also, the fact that there was no sexual abuse, rather the body was recomposed, makes sense. More than one, I don't think so. Generally, the number of criminals goes against preserving evidence."

"True, I also think it's just one person. No clues left, meticulous, appropriate, organized, and above all, carefully orchestrated the crime."

"Let's get some rest for a few hours; my brain is smoking, I need to rest."

"Right on, buddy! Good idea! Your brain processes data while you sleep; you wake up, and you have a lead!"

"Smitty, you're truly an angel from Heaven, always well-prepared. Merry Christmas! Go home to your kids."

"Okay, Adam, bye, James! I'll lock up after you guys leave!"

Once in the car, James looked at me, ready to speak but holding back.

"Tell me, should I take you home?"

"At the station, I have the department car. I'll go with that. My wife is waiting, thanks."

"You're a real good man, one of those priceless ones. I mean it from the heart."

"And you, Detective? Anyone waiting for you?"

That's what he wanted to ask.

"Unfortunately, no. Too many stories ended badly. The disappointment was so intense that it made me forget the few moments of ecstasy."

"Eve Bloom..."

"Yes, I like her. I'm a professional, though. I'll protect her, probably save her life, and then when everything is over, I'll court her. You can count on it," and I smiled.

"Merry Christmas, Detective!" and he got out of the car.

I opened the door to my apartment; it was literally freezing. The boiler had broken a few days ago, and I hadn't had time to get it fixed. It was a nice apartment, except for the fact that the subway woke me up every time I managed to sleep. A single man's apartment, essential, functional, and excessively clean. My cat kept me company. A large male Chartreux, with a powerful head that made him resemble a lion more than a cat. He came over sleepily; I kept him indoors, fearing that some local Chinese might mistake him for a steamed dumpling filling. I opened a can of tuna and natural hake for him.

"I know, you're my only weakness. Come on, big kitty, eat and grow big and strong!"

I stroked his head, and I clearly heard his purrs at their best. I loved him; he kept me company, was harmless and gentle, altruistic for a solitary cat, and although neutered, absolutely masculine. He resembled me; he was, in fact, my animal alter ego upon which I poured my unconditional love. I had taken him as a kitten, and now, at the venerable age of almost twelve, I could say that we were a formidable couple.

I slumped onto the leather sofa, closed my eyes. I was tired. The image of the hanging girl haunted my memory. My legs felt light and numb, my mind fluid and fast. The floor around me had liquefied, taking on a gelatinous consistency, and my feet sank into the dense sludge that was now my rented parquet. A voice hissed in my ear, a voice that was an imperceptibly human grunt, probably animal.

"It was demonic today, wasn't it?"

"Yes," I replied politely, intimidated by the authoritative superiority of that inhuman sound.

"I can do worse, you know? I can conceive more images of more shocking entities and allow you to reach solutions only to make your deduction vanish as if it were the faint beat of a butterfly."

"Why?" The sludge engulfed me up to my calves; my body was heavy and laden, laden and breathless from the terrible images I had seen so far. Violated women, men with severed limbs, blood, viscera, excrement. The end could really be resolved in a matter of fluids and disordered and malodorous masses. And of deplorable appearance.

"Why does the child get on the Ferris wheel? Why does he wait for presents at Christmas? Why does he long to have cotton candy bought for him?"

"Do I have to answer? Did I speak?" Yet something had come out of my mouth.

"Because it is in their simple and innocent nature, and so it is in my nature to do what I am capable of and what I was created for. If I didn't exist, there would be no child waiting for Christmas night. If I didn't exist, the Ferris wheel wouldn't have been created to observe the world from above and delight in the city lights."

"I don't understand. I feel immobilized... was it you?"

"Me?" he chuckled. "You're giving me too much power."

"What do you want? Who are you?"

"I am your friend, your best friend. Follow me, and you will be free. Follow me, and you will have no doubts. I will guide you."

"Where?"

"Where your nature takes you."

I tried to open my eyelids, sharpen my vision in the dark, perceive and identify smells, and then the snout of a wild boar and the acrid smell of a stable and dung appeared before me. A low, prolonged roar woke me because it was my cat growling at me, with his fur standing on end, crouched ready to pounce, and his tail puffed up and straight.

I blinked; I already didn't remember anything, and in the end, I had rested. Only a faint smell of dung in the air prompted me to open the windows slightly. Getting up, I realized that I could move without any problem and discarded all memories because it was already dawn, and after a quick cold shower, a long morning awaited me.

The Mall – Central – Southern part of Central Park

Date: December 25, 2023

Time: 9:14 AM

Adam observed the bare trees along the avenue. Daylight made spirits brighter and more serene, quieter. For a late December day, it was unusually warm. A pale sun tried to break through the morning fog and smog. He gazed at the sun, deciding to divert towards Eve Bloom's residence for a quick reconnaissance, putting on his sunglasses.

He had completely changed his clothes, except for the inseparable Nikes. He protected himself further with a snowboarder's wool hat.

The building was silent, no passersby, a few taxis sped along the avenue. Even the concierge was absent, probably due to the holidays. Eve's mailbox was empty. Still empty. He waited, grabbed a long coffee with a hint of cinnamon and milk from the nearby bar, and stood at the street corner with a perfect view.

The newspaper delivery boy on a skateboard passed by. But he didn't stop. Apparently, there were few readers in that Victorian building. The streets began to fill up, but the mailbox was still empty.

Suddenly, the front door opened from the inside. A tall and sinuous blonde wearing a fur hat, large dark glasses, and a fur coat worthy of a diva came out.

It was Eve. She had a white envelope in her gloved hand. He approached her. Why? He wouldn't have wanted to find out that she wasn't cooperating with the police, so he made it easier for her to face him.

"Miss Bloom?" he called.

She woke up disoriented. "I was coming to you... were you following me?" she regretted, clearly resentful, and therefore innocent.

"Pedinare has a modern structure in verb formation, but it comes from the Latin sequor, which indeed means to follow behind. However, I wasn't following you because you just came out. If anything, I was waiting for you without disturbing, giving you the opportunity to be a good citizen effortlessly," I clarified.

"I don't know why you were waiting for me, but here's the letter and the new riddle."

"Waiting, in fact, derives from expecto, meaning to await anxiously outside, more or less where I was, with my coffee, which is very good. Come, I'll offer you one, and meanwhile, let's see this clue. Did you open it with leather gloves?"

"I took the envelope without gloves, but I didn't open anything. Then I put on gloves as I usually do in winter and took the envelope again."

"So, presumably, there are three types of fingerprints: yours, the delivery boy's, and the killer's," Eve shivered.

I felt sorry for her, but it was the truth. "Why don't you think there are only two?" she smiled.

I understood at that moment that she liked me. It was both a question and not, a bridge to cross and a landing strip to make her comfortable with my opinion, a way to flatter me and submit to my viewpoint, using the all-female cunning of the beautiful woman. She was adorable, an adorable conqueror.

I smiled back at her, showing my teeth and slightly pronounced canines because in the act, I wanted to bite her neck and arms and devour her with the passion I already felt for her.

"A killer so cautious that he leaves no prints or traces of himself hardly delivers the letter in person. He must have brought it to him at night. Where was he?"

"He slid it under the door, should we open it?"

I put on gloves. The usual anonymous white paper, TNR 12,

"In the realm of darkness,

silence reigns supreme.

They are millions, but only one is the glove.

Among the golden stars, it holds a secret.

Very ancient, but it concludes in eternity."

I handed her the sheet. "Don't touch it; I'll hold it, then we'll take it to the forensic team together. Unfortunately, you might have to identify the body."

She looked at me alarmed. "No no no... I don't have to do anything..."

"In the meantime, read it and give me the solution. If they sent it to you, it seems you can decipher it."

"In truth, I had a dream, and I dreamt the word. Certainly, when I woke up this morning, it had no meaning, but now I believe it's like this... It's the Milky Way. The Milky Way could be the name of a venue, a place to gather tonight at 6:00 PM," she said laconically.

"You're beautiful and intelligent. Why does a woman like you accept gifts and benefits in exchange for friendship? You can have everything..."

She looked straight into my eyes. Her eyes were covered by dark lenses, but I could sense her disapproval. She disapproved of my moralism and ethics.

"Is it a problem?"

I smiled. No, it wasn't really a problem. She smiled too.

"So, can we become lovers without you being incredibly jealous and making me give up all my benefits?"

I seriously considered it.

"No."

"So, do I have to leave them and live in your apartment?"

I nodded.

She seriously thought about it for a few seconds. "I want a kiss before deciding whether to leave my penthouse."

"Take off your sunglasses. You're beautiful; I want to see your face."

She obeyed. My heart accelerated its beats; it was an organ detached from me. I was excited and subservient, anxious and eager at the same time, fearful and excited.

I took her face in my hands and devoured her mouth. She eagerly opened up, allowing my tongue in. We embraced passionately; I rubbed my erection against her stomach. She pulled me closer and gasped, breaking away.

I had never experienced such passion, as if I had entered a fast and spasmodic vortex, sensual and mysterious, where only my senses were undisputed masters.

"Please, can you say my name? I want to hear you pronounce it with your soft voice," I said gently, caressing her face with rough fingertips.

"I don't know your name..." she smiled, showing her white and well-maintained teeth.

"Adam."

"Adam..."

"Mmmm, I would be incredibly jealous..."

"I can imagine. Okay, I accept, but you'll have to be patient; the first times will be difficult. I'm used to a lot."

"Gifts, privileges, trips?"

"Parties, clothes, jewelry..." she added, ecstatically smiling.

"They present you like a painting or a car or new hardware... you know?"

"Of course! But my dignity is intact. I feel like a clever little fox..."

Adam held her tightly; she was his. No trips, no jewelry that wasn't purchased within his means.

"Eve, you are a beautiful woman, and I understand that beauty for some arouses possessiveness. For me, it's not like that. You touched my heart, for that tear that you could hardly hold back last night, and in the end, it slipped down your cheek without you realizing. Because I understand that you are a complicated woman in whom one can get lost. I want to lose myself with you, joyfully," and he moved his hand to her cheek, caressing it with rough fingertips.

She sighed. "The past doesn't serve us. It's not useful; it's been. We can have the future."

Adam nodded. "I want to kiss you again and hold you, but I also have to take you to the station to identify your sister's body, ask you some questions, understand why and to what extent you are involved."

She shivered at the word "body." "Yes, I understand. You need to know the venue where they gather to defend me, right?"

"Yes, I'm afraid you're more involved than we initially thought. It's not normal for these letters to arrive, and they were, of the same type, at the crime scene. Do you understand?"

"Do you want to know how long I've been receiving them?"

"You already told us. Since you got divorced."

"Yes, more or less. My job is centered around relationships. This was a way to have them, and I quickly climbed the career ladder."

"It surely had its price."

"Is it the epitaph on my tomb?" she asked with a nervous laugh.

"No. As long as I'm alive, no," and he hugged her again, embracing her tenderly.

"Let's go to your place, just a second, ten minutes. Life slips away without us being able to slow it down. I don't know how the day will proceed, and I would like to remember this moment forever, or at least until evening."

"Until 6:00 PM."

"Right..."

I smiled at her, a long smile, one of those I reserved for special people, sincere, true, amiable. It was the smile I captured on my cat's soul when I gave him his favorite food, when I left him the blanket to lie on warmly, when diligently petting him while he purred magnanimously. It was the smile of affection that asked for affection in return.

"Come, I also want you," she said.

"Is it very easy?" I commented, following her.

"Yes, strangely easy. I don't understand why. Usually, all relationships go through a standard time of habit and acceptance. We seem to have reset this moment to enjoy each other." She was climbing the stairs, and I watched her back covered by the long coat, her thin ankles joined by expensive heels.

She opened the door and entered. I followed her and closed it behind me. The silence was almost alarming. Dim light dominated the elegant living room. The marble, just covered by wool carpets, muffled her steps.

She took off her coat, glasses, hat.

I stood motionless by the door of his house, like the fox who is deciding to trust but the headlights blind him and it would not seem a good idea, to proceed.

She wore black wool pants, unfastened them at the waist and slid them down her long legs.

Her white lace panties burned my pupils. She casually crossed her hands over the flaps of her black sweater and lifted them over her head, to quickly pull it away, tossing it over the beige couch.

Her bra barely covered her nipples, which I glimpsed beneath the lace rising like soldiers ready to attack.

My breathing had become labored.

How long had it been?

"Stand there?" he taunted me.

I could not look away from the white breasts, a few blond strands had trapped themselves deliberately in the hollow between the breasts.

I shook my head, the saliva had left me.

I moved closer.

As soon as I was within her reach, she removed my raincoat.

"That's better, isn't it?"

I stopped her hands; she was about to take off my sweater, too.

"You're too used to getting your own way, aren't you?"

I could feel the rapid beat of her blood racing through the veins of her clenched wrists.

She instinctively closed her hands into fists.

I brought them behind her back, holding her steady with one hand and forcing her to arch toward my pelvis with hers.

My erection was already at its peak.

I pulled at the lace of her briefs, which gave way and broke.

I pushed her against the table, she would have fallen but I resisted her, in a few steps she leaned her buttocks against the cold wood.

"Let go of my wrists, I don't like being held like this..."

"I guess that's not true, you have to get used to a man."

I unzipped my pants and as I spread her legs with mine, I pulled out my turgid member to thrust it into her.

I found her moist and warm, perfectly ready.

She gasped and shuddered. Her legs came up and grazed my hips.

"Push it in me detective..." she whispered in my ear, her voice warm and soft, arched with pleasure.

Beginning to thrust intensely, she responded with the arousal in her voice.

I could feel her enjoying, he let go of her wrists and hung onto me, taking my mouth and taking me on top of her.

Feeling her orgasm rising, I released her breasts, squeezing one of them. It was firm and soft, velvety and firm, moving rhythmically with us at my strokes. When I took her nipple between my forefinger and thumb, she felt her uterus contract and release. Her scream involved me, her vagina released its sour humors, I followed, letting my pleasure explode violently inside her.

I also screamed through clenched teeth. I ejaculated with force and power, then collapsed with my body, drained, onto her.

Silence enveloped us like a woolen blanket.

In the shadows a red, demonic figure with animal features stared at us, enjoying our bestiality.

"Bravo, bravo...you are an orgasm for my grrrr eyes..."

CHAPTER FIVE

86TH St Transvers Rd, New York, NY 10024

Date: December 25, 2023

Time: 12:04 AM

The police station was swarming with scum. Christmas inspired the area's worst gangs to crime.

They made their way through the melee at the entrance, while some colleagues waved, watching them together.

A policeman could not help but miss it, his hand affectionately holding her hand. Him making his way through, leaving space for her. He who genuinely involved looked at her to make sure that that great confusion, did not frighten her.

They took refuge in the office.

James opened the door a few minutes later, without knocking.

"Detective News!"

He pointed to Eve.

"Is the young lady here for body identification and questioning?"

"I honestly don't think I'll see any dead body," Eve interjected.

"No, I'd let it go, although it's procedure and you're right, some clues might emerge, but the young lady hasn't seen her sister in years, maybe she doesn't remember any particular signs or anything else that might come to our aid. So let's overlook it, instead, tell me the news."

"Another body has been found, of a homeless man, dressed as Santa Claus. Apparently dead from overdose, but forensics will confirm or not the hasty diagnosis...."

"I see no news...."

"The news is that he had a letter pinned on his red jacket....addressed to you."

"To me??" I leapt to my feet sharply, the hairs on the back of my neck standing upright and alert, my senses alert.

Now I understood why James had not knocked before entering.

"Shall we let the young lady out?" he asked hesitantly in fact.

"No, she also received a letter...she might as well help us."

James handed me the plastic that contained the A4 sheet with the nursery rhyme.

"In the secret twilight, where the sun disappears,

Two destinies entwined, in the darkness to shine.

They seek each other secretly, among unknown paths,

Where taboo reveals stories, of minute passions.

Under the shadow of a remote and discreet place,

Glances cross, in a perfect union.

Between whispers and caresses, in the telling darkness,

Who are they, in this dance that breaks through?"

I blinked twice.

I handed the paper to Eve.

She read and looked at me strangely.

"What time was the body found?" I asked, but I knew the answer.

"The death seems to be placed from 3:00 AM to 8:00 AM."

Taking the paper back, I turned it over.

In clear, cursive letters, I read my name.

Noises from the hallway filled the air. No one dared to breathe.

"Is there anything I don't know, Detective?"

"No, nothing!"

"If we have to protect you, it would be better to know!"

"James, no. It's under control!" but a drop of sweat beaded on my forehead.

Eve let herself fall into a wooden chair.

"Here's the other letter, they're meeting in a place that resembles the Milky Way in name, look up the possible combinations with the computer. We are going to the morgue, I must get more details about the death of the homeless man."

"He was homeless, an anonymous man."

"Have you identified him?"

"At the registry, Lucas Shade, known among his fellow street dwellers as Seraph, 53 years old, alcoholic, without family, without a home."

I fell silent; something was escaping me, but it was there for me to see.

"Lucas, from the Greek Loukas, Latin Lux, light. Shade from shadow, darkness. Seraph, angel. Angel of light and darkness. Refers to both Hell and Paradise. Which one, though?"

"I believe both," Eve whispered.

We both, James and I, looked at her, astonished.

"Think about the nursery rhyme, the lovers. The lovers who meet before Paradise and Hell, who are they? Who are the first lovers?"

She said it all in one breath, with a growing fear in her voice, looking me straight in the eyes. I saw her pupils widen and dull with fear.

"Adam and Eve..." James completed.

An angelic voice whispered in my ear: "Stop, linger..." I tried to ignore the dizziness rising within me at those words. I had to act! James pressed on with his peremptory manner:

"You can't stay on this case, Adam! I'm telling you as a friend! You absolutely can't; you need a guard and be separated from her!"

I ran my hand through my hair.

"Stop! Everything is still being built from here; choose wisely..."

Beside me, I felt a presence inconsistent and rarefied, incorporeal but of powerful energy with long blonde braids and bird wings. I sighed and spoke to myself and the others.

"Yes, we should do that, it's evident. He wants this, or maybe not. He knows we'll be together, and you'll keep silent and go check the meeting place. Because the alternative is to separate us, take us to two opposite countries under guard, and forget about catching this deviant and psychopathic liar who's having fun with us! He already knows that I want to catch him and that I'll do it my way... He has already calculated

that I'll only protect her because I'm convinced
I'm a hero and, above all, an invincible hero...
So, do you know what we'll do?"

"Adam, it seems obvious!"

"Yes, prepare a car and a guard. She'll be taken
to a place even I shouldn't know, under guard.
This must happen immediately."

"Yes, and you?"

"Me too, divide us and keep an eye on us. It's
what he doesn't expect us to do because it's the
simplest solution."

"Okay, and for tonight, who do we send?"

"Nobody. He's waiting for that too. He won't strike there. He wants us. He can strike anywhere, but in the end, he wants us. So, he won't act tonight if we disappear. He'll need time to organize and find other victims."

"It makes sense. Meanwhile, we understand the connection because of you two, and I honestly think it all starts with the girl."

James pointed his finger at Eve.

The white bird wings grabbed Eve like a shield. She was protected, evidently. It was the right path!

"Yes, while we make her disappear, you really have to check every friendship, every movement of hers. I'm sorry, Eve, it's necessary."

James took Eve's arm gently.

"Follow me; I'll take you to your apartment to get some clothes."

"Oh God, is my life radically changing? Am I going to be sent to a remote corner of America and forgotten?"

"We really have to; it's dangerous to keep you here. We can't do it; you're really risking your life," I told her gently.

I looked at her again and again in the blue eyes, the color of crystal-clear streams. I wanted to imprint her angelic face in my mind to never forget it.

"Now it's my turn," I whispered as they closed the door. I picked up the phone: "Commander Murray? Yes, this is Detective Jones, Adam Jones. I need an armed escort; I'm certain I'm the next target of a killer. Yes, yes, you guessed it, the Christmas case, the Observatory, the girl, yes, of course, Susan Bloom. Okay, okay, good, I'll wait here in my office. Thank you," and I hung up.

"I had to make another phone call... 'Forensics? Yes, Smitty? Are you still there with your buddies?... yes, I know, packed at Christmas! Tell me about the homeless guy? What did you find on him?... I figured, can you send me a picture? I'd like to see the evidence. In the rectum? ... how deep? ... Okay, got it... a picture, please. Anything else I need to know?... No, okay... what's happening? As usual... a lot of dust... but this time it seems they want me... Give me the picture! Thank you! You're my favorite mortuary angel!' I hung up. The photo arrived on my phone. I downloaded it, eager. Before my eyes was a sheriff's star. A sheriff's star like the ones you wear at Carnival with a cowboy costume. The star was inserted into the rectum of the homeless man's corpse. A boar's grunt reached me. I turned my head behind me. The wall with its mugshots answered me. There was nothing. It was my imagination. I went to the computer; I had to know where they would meet tonight at 6:00 PM. Milky way, milky way... there was a Broadway agency, a Korean restaurant, a bowling alley, an ice cream shop, a fast-food joint... the most likely was the Korean restaurant. I wrote down the address: 3626A Union St, Queens, NY, 11354. I sent the message to James. There was a knock. It was my escort. 'Agents... Merry Christmas! Where are you taking me?'"

Chevrolet Impala at the traffic light at West 66th Street and Central Park West

Date: December 25, 2023

Time: 12:56 AM

James drove the official car, a Chevrolet Impala with few years and few kilometers, determined not to take the woman to the apartment but directly hand her over to the chosen protection team.

That apartment was evidently under surveillance; there was no use fooling oneself that the killer couldn't enter or leave or even that there weren't cameras scattered around to monitor the girl. He glanced at her. She was anxious, twisting her hands in her lap, gripping her wool coat, staring out the side window.

 The perfect and haughty profile reminded him of those '50s divas, famous for their untouchable beauty.

"Relax, we'll protect you. I've decided not to take you to the apartment. If you have plants, pets, or anything else, tell a friend now, saying you'll be away for a while, a study vacation, or a solo trip."

Eve turned sharply towards the policeman.

"I have no plants, nor animals, but I'd like my toothbrush and my underwear for the trip, as you call it, study..."

"I don't trust it. That apartment is a hunting ground." James sighed, continuing.

"I don't know what happened with Adam and how far you've gone together, but evidently, the killer saw you. So, he'll understand that I don't trust entering a place with cameras or microphones to communicate our moves..."

He emphasized the word 'moves.' She sighed. "I don't believe anyone would want to kill me. Or hurt me with torture or something; I'm a peaceful woman, I love parties and beautiful clothes, and I've never quarreled with anyone..."

"A rejected lover, a jealous boyfriend, a vindictive husband. You have no idea how the human mind deviates when subjected to the right stimuli."

After passing the traffic light, the Chevrolet turned right. The square nose bounced slightly over a road pothole; the suspensions gave a small warning of control. It was traveling at 30 km/h. The automatic transmission was set to Drive, James pressed the gear pedal, accelerating to 45 km/h. The road was clear; it was lunchtime, Christmas called its followers into the privacy of their metropolitan homes. The timer triggered at 50 km/h. It was positioned between the front arms and the suspension springs, stopped with high-temperature insulating tape. The wires ran to a capsule 30 cm in size, ovoid in shape, the detonator, containing a small amount of highly flammable nitroglycerin. Next to the detonator, taped with wide yellow adhesive tape, was the dynamite. The dynamite was composed of 60% sulfuric acid and 20% nitric acid, reinforced by strong nitric acid. It ignited with a small combustion, given by the heat generated by the detonator explosion. The heat from the Chevrolet's engine and the gasoline tank contributed to a perfect spread.

 "Strange that a beautiful woman like you hasn't sown some disappointed admirers..."

"Don't do this to me! I have no disappointed lovers because I live a normal life, and if I don't want to, I say it clearly!"

"Normal life? Are you kidding? Here in this city?"

Eve felt like there were three of them in the cabin. She didn't know how to bring up the topic, but she was sure that among them in the back seat, a little girl with long blonde braids was sitting.

"Eve, slow down..."

She didn't understand, Eve. She felt protected, though.

James applied a firmer pressure on the gear pedal; he was getting nervous. The road was clear; this lady seemed high-handed enough to denigrate more than one admirer. As a child, he remembered the films of Grace Kelly; she was beautiful in black and white, with that face of perfect features as she watched Cary Grant slide across French roofs.

They heard a bang, very close, under their feet, then the flames invaded the cabin. James felt an enormous heat on his legs and thought he wouldn't have children. He steered the car to stop it against any wall on the side of the road, to collide and stop, the only chance to get out of the vehicle's blazing march. The flames licked their clothes, skimmed their skin; smoke and heat infiltrated the airways, their eyes burned, Eve's hair took on the appearance of a medieval torch. Then the second detonation tore the car, bodies, limbs apart.

James felt the sensation of spreading, liquefying; he was wrong, there was no chance of surviving a bomb. Eve had already lost consciousness. Her head hung like a burning puppet on the sides of the body. Someone used the fire hose against them.

The force of the water created an opening on the passenger side. Daring hands pulled the girl out; James thought, better this way, I die a hero, they'll glorify me on a silver memorial plaque for the commendable years of service. In the end, it's better to die than survive at the New York Burn Center, probably without the use of legs; the explosion had hit them squarely, and he felt the bones shatter from the inside and tear the flesh of the calves and ankles.

His last thought was for his yellow budgie, alone in his cage. He hoped the neighbor would adopt him and that the picture he had given on his card to the department was really horrible and they would probably use that one at his memorial because it was the only one they owned.

He was no longer breathing, his lungs collapsed, laden with burns, his heart slowly decelerating its beats. Indistinct noises, screams. A siren.

"Hurry the stretcher! There is a pulse! Intubate!"

The ambulance headed with sirens blaring toward Mount Sinai Hospital.

Eve was still breathing, albeit with very severe burns to her airway and on her body.

"IV!"

"I can't find a vein..." anxiously replied the female paramedic. (Gertrude of German descent on her maternal grandmother's side, a square big woman with short blond hair and icy eyes that hurt as soon as they landed on you. Single, probably an unexpressed lesbian, with no children and a dog peeing in the house).

Let me do it, or else the Princess here leaves to visit her dead ancestors!" (Patrick, half-Indian, half-Irish, penitent alcoholic, single by choice, fucking hot in boxers and with an unexpressed passion for George Clooney)

"Here's vein found, looks solid, IV started, 2 min. on arrival, communicate with Hospital, top priority, have them prep the OR!"

"Yeah ok!" (Jeff, driving, married with twin toddlers, wife had been cheating on him for some time, even the paternity of the children was in question, but they were so beautiful he was ready to forgive any betrayal...)

Mount Sinai Hospital, acceptance

Date: Dec. 25, 2023

Time: 1:18 PM

"The Princess is slipping away, faster, go faster!" Patrick was convinced that the Princess needed to be saved, not realizing like Gertrude that perhaps this woman, once probably beautiful and charming, would not have withstood a life with a burned face and a mangled body.

"She's already in the operating room; it's done! Good job! I'm sure they'll save her!"

Gertrude responded loudly, shamelessly lying. In her heart, she hoped that the woman would die loaded with morphine, so doped up that she wouldn't realize she had left this world, blown up inside a police Chevrolet on Christmas morning. The doors of the operating room closed in front of them, the stretcher with Eve, or what was left of her, was already in the operating room in the presence of a young surgeon still in training, with a very long shift behind him, a lot of coffee in his system, and an unhealthy desire to do the right thing. Two gigantic wings, white with swan feathering, spread in the corridor; a little girl took flight. Her job there was done.

Central Park Police District, Office of Detective Adam Jones.

Date: December 25, 2023

Time: 1:18 PM

The phone rang. "Answer it, Adam," grunted his foul-smelling host.

Adam stared at the phone; it rang for emergencies or news conveyed by his superiors.

"Hello?"

"Commander? Yes...Eve Bloom? Yes, she was escorted by the chosen police officer James Patterson...NO! Oh my God! James? ...Oh my God!...The...girl? No, oh no, really? At Mount Sinai Hospital...okay, no, I'm truly speechless, a blow! I liked James; he was a good companion. Okay, yes, no, he had no one, family? I don't know...okay, under guard, I'm waiting for them...I want to go to the Hospital, can I?...No, I understand, okay, immediately under guard. Okay, thank you, Sir."

I put my hands on my face, slumping into the wooden chair. Eve between life and death,

James dead, blown up with a bomb placed on the patrol car.

There was a knock.

"Yes."

"Detective, we are Agents Louis and Vermont; we are here to escort you to a safe place."

Two well-built agents, perhaps excessively muscular, positioned themselves between me and the door.

The safe place was an apartment in Brooklyn used to hold important witnesses. A common apartment, on an ordinary street with a single entrance and two windows, on the third floor of a building for the elderly.

"Yes, okay, I'm ready, but I wanted to stop by Mount Sinai to find out if the girl will make it. I really care."

"The Commander ordered us to go directly to the safe place," replied Louis.

"She won't run away, and you will always be with me. I know what the Commander said, but I care about that girl. I'm devastated, and James...try to understand."

"We follow orders, Detective. That's why we're alive," Agent Vermont repeated.

"Okay, I'll follow you; you've convinced me," I stood up and led them to the door.

The apartment was located in Bay Ridge, Brooklyn, NY, 15421. The car journey was quite dull. The two officers occupied the front seats, and I sat in the back. The car glided on the asphalt at a moderate speed. I thought about Eve, about her body. A knot tightened in my stomach.

Guilt, suffering, pity. Did I want her to stay alive? No.

"No, you don't want that... think about it!" a flutelike voice whispered behind me.

Actually, no. She was right. Here was the stone-faced building decorated with stone embellishments. The three steps at the entrance, the wooden door, the iron railing. Some curious glances through the slightly parted curtains.

They parked the car. Vermont turned toward me. I noticed his brown eyes veined with curious golden specks, extremely full lips, and an aquiline nose. I was wearing a Yankees cap with the visor; he lifted it slightly, scratched his forehead, and I could glimpse his very short, almost shaved hair.

"Detective, we go in first, and then Louis will come to get you. It's the procedure." I nodded.

"I'll wait here. Is there coffee inside?"

Louis stopped the car and chuckled. "What a Christmas, huh, boss?"

They both got out. They scanned the street to the right and left; it was deserted. I noticed the Glock in Vermont's holster; he winked at me from its cold, fiber-reinforced polymer grip.

"I'm here," it said. "I am the Law."

Next to me, sitting comfortably, a boar of enormous proportions occupied the entire back seat. It stared at me with restless and dominant red eyes.

"Make yourself comfortable, friend," his voice was primitive and guttural. They were sounds, but I understood them perfectly. They were unmoving sounds that tore through the air and made it saturated with a nauseating odor. The two disappeared into the building's vestibule. Their disappearance from my sight brought me back to reality.

Third Floor, Bay Ridge Brooklyn NY, 15421

Date: December 25, 2023

Time: 2:18 PM

Vermont observed the third floor. Apparently, everything seemed in order, silent, deserted. He signaled to Louis. They had been partners for four years in special escorts, accustomed to high-risk situations. Uncomfortable witnesses to protect, mobsters, politicians' prostitutes, drugs, and now even dark movies. They handed them over with top priority, uncomfortable to keep alive until their testimonies or until they negotiated their freedom. To be honest, few made it.

Louis was a good companion, reliable, generous, and an excellent shooter even from 5 meters with a lightweight Feinwerkbau 800. Vermont sniffed the gas just before entering the door. Louis was inside and turned to him with an annoyed expression. His hand was on the light switch.

"NOOOOOOOOOOOOOOOOOOOOOOOOOOOOOOOOOOOOOOOOOOOO,"

Vermont shouted, but it was too late. The light bulb turned on, the air was saturated with gas, and the impact was devastating. Louis flew against the vestibule wall with his ribcage broken in multiple places, two ligament injuries, and both ribs cracked. Vermont suffered the rebound of the explosion diagonally, flew off the stairs, only breaking his ribs and right leg. The fire re-entered after the blast; they had used only methane gas for the explosion, triggered by the tungsten wire of the light bulb, made incandescent.

The window panes violently fell onto the Dodge Police car parked on the side of the road. Adam jerked, hurriedly got out of the car, and covering his face with a flap of his raincoat, climbed the stairs of the building. He found Vermont in an abnormal position on the first-floor stairs. He felt his jugular.

He was alive. Louis a little higher emitted guttural sounds similar to a request for help.

"Calm down; I'll call the paramedics and the police!"

He went back down the stairs.

Vermont couldn't have heard it, unconscious. Louis was too busy suffering.

He returned to the car, took the driver's seat. The keys to the Dodge were perfectly inserted.

He started the car.

CHAPTER SIX

Mount Sinai Hospital, Major Burn Center

Date: December 25, 2023

Time: 1:56 PM

Adam entered the ward. The silence was absolute. The vinyl floors slid beneath the rubber of my Nike shoes. I felt tired. The raincoat partially covered me, concealing the Glock. An eager nurse approached me. Behind her, angelic wings touched the boundaries of the corridor, white and luminous as if lit from within with LED bulbs. She whispered,

"You can't stay here; it's a restricted area, and you need authorization to stay or talk to one of the doctors."

"I'm a cop,"

I showed her the badge with the serial number. "Ah, a detective... I understand. What can I do for you?"

"I'd like to get news about Eve Bloom. She was admitted here following an explosion she was involved in."

"Yes, Miss Bloom arrived about an hour ago. She underwent surgery. Now she's stable. Any relatives that you know of?"

"No, she has no relatives."

She was alone.

"What does stable mean?"

"It means she's in a deep sedation, with severe burns on her body, damaged lungs, and a fractured left leg... if you want, I can call the doctor who operated on her."

"No... no... I understand she won't regain consciousness soon, right?"

"She's in critical condition; we doubt she'll make it through the day. I can inform you if there are any changes."

Game over then.

Eve Bloom was game over, in critical condition, ergo, she's about to die, but we try our best to do our job for which we studied for many years and for which we applied ourselves tirelessly, and we've pumped her so full of morphine that if, by chance, she survives, she would, of course, be addicted. The angelic wings closed protectively around the nurse's body like a shield. I glimpsed two blonde braids behind the woman's figure and a slender child's body.

"Can I see her?"

I whispered, looking at my white Nikes and the color contrast with the hospital's blue vinyl floor. A long yellow line ran along the corridor to a double-door without locks.

"She's in the intensive care unit to protect her from bacteria. You can see her through glass. The bed is only accessible to the service staff. I believe the young lady can't help you right now. If you'll excuse me, I have to ask you to leave the ward."

"Leave the ward... okay, yes, fine, thank you."

I stared at her astonished (shocked); her brown eyes were cold, a nonchalant Hispanic woman. I had no choice; I left the hospital. The meeting with the enigmatic group was scheduled for 6:00 PM, about 3 hours away. Assuming the rendezvous point was the Korean restaurant, I needed to conduct a reconnaissance.

The hypothesis that it wasn't one killer but more than one was starting to emerge in my speculative mind.

"Grrrr, come in... it's cold outside... grrrr,"

who was whispering to me? Who was growling? I investigated the space around me, left and right. I saw nothing. Just an unhealthy smell of sewage wafted into my nostrils. I climbed onto the Dodge; the interior was comfortable.

 I let my gaze wander in the hospital parking lot, cluttered with utility vehicles.

I stopped my mind, forcing it to reflect.

The bombs were evidently already in place.

The Killer knew that we would head in two separate directions, anticipating every reasoning of mine, surpassing me in speed and discernment. He knew. Two bombs like that must be placed. For James's car bomb, he must have used the nighttime hours, a targeted placement time of about 30 minutes, maybe 45 minutes if he was particularly meticulous. To saturate the air with methane gas, on the other hand, it certainly took about 3 hours, maybe 4. So, the whole morning.

Why target James?

To get to Eve, perhaps. Who was the real target? Susan Bloom was the first victim.

An unknown, unfamiliar, and insignificant girl. Eve was probably the second intended victim, and James was the accidental one.

But would I be the third victim? There was no connection. It was chaos, entropy. He observed people getting into cars, performing careful reverse maneuvers, driving away, and others arriving and occupying marked spaces.

A balanced ecosystem. Balanced.

A memory made its way into my mind. Something James had said once, about the balance on which the interpretation of the Law is based.

The interpretation that we quickly make when faced with danger. The balance of divergence. What was the killer's goal?

"Say yes!"

Who was it? Who's there? A delicate voice enticed me. Say yes... YES!

To what? Now let me think... It was becoming clear in my mind that the goal was a demonstration of strength and intellect.

The antagonist was the Police, the Law, the Law Enforcement, indiscriminately.

Susan Bloom was bait, the first one, an ordinary woman to attract our attention.

They were all anonymous people, even Eve, not connected to each other, except for the accidental relationship.

The homeless man, James, the two cops Vermont and Louis, accidental, like pawns on a chessboard.

These accidental deaths, however, were meant to signify cunning, calculation, premeditation;

they were "balanced," like message-laden travelers.

Messages addressed to whom?

I started the Dodge, the engine vibrated and roared excitedly.

I headed toward The Korean Restaurant.

It was imperative to be present at the meeting.

I would have to give justifications to my Commander, several phone calls had appeared on my phone display that I had deliberately ignored.

"Bravo grrr! That's the way I like you!Tenacious meat! Grrr!"

The usual mephitic odor permeated the air as if a major, foul-smelling fart had been cast beside me.

Eve's face appeared in my memories, my stomach contracted in a demonic grip.

Game over for Eve Bloom.

Milky Way, 3626°, Union Street, Queens, NY 11354

Date: December 25, 2023

Time: 15:12 PM

I crossed the threshold of the small Korean-style restaurant. Rough ceramic floors, wooden walls, plastic tables, and adorable Christmas placemats as place markers.

An unassuming eatery with a fried smell soaked to the white faux-cotton curtains.

I approached the counter, a small, thin Korean man ranging in age from 40 to 50, with a hint of a mustache above his thin upper lip, apostrophized me in Korean.

I stared at him, actually understanding.

He was telling me that they were closed and that I had to leave.

"Detective...police..." I flashed my badge.

His expression changed from annoyed to alarmed. They were probably not up to various hygiene standards judging by the level of whiteness of the curtains hanging in the windows.

"English?"

"We all right!"

Disappearing behind a sliding door, the smell of grease and pickled vegetables reached my nostrils, nauseating me.

Again Eve's face peeped into my memory.

The Korean man re-entered followed by a younger boy, surely naturalized judging by the snow-white Jordans and casual overalls he sported.

"My father asks what you want?" he was deferential and respectful.

"Are you planning an event tonight? With several guests? At 6 p.m.? Maybe you have a room reserved for such things, a prive?"

"Yes, tonight we booked the second floor with the typical dinner to a group, they are control aspects, do you want to know how many people are?"

"Yes please..."

"12 people."

"They have been here before, do you know them?"

"No, I don't think so, the name of the reservation doesn't tell me anything."

"Does it tell me?"

"Mr. Theodore Alphonse."

"Actually he told me to set the table for 13 but that only 12 would dine, it was his explicit request."

"You spoke to him directly?"

"Yes...but that's all I remember..."

"The tone of voice, how old could he have been? He was educated, he had accents...try to remember..."

The boy stared blankly for a few seconds.

"No, he was absolutely anonymous, concise and with this request I told you. She had no preference on the menu, no problem on the price, she only had this request...as I told her."

"I get it but it's important...the 13th person why would she not have dinner, did you explain it to her?"

"No. Only pay for 12 people but want an extra cover."

For the dead man or the killer, I thought.

I scratched my forehead. I was tired and anxious, I had to let three hours pass, the wait would be nerve-racking, away from the Police, away from friends, away from ...

Game over for Eve.

Best to remember.

"Okay thanks see you tonight. I think there will be 14 of us at the end ..."

I called my commander, I was liable to prosecution for insubordination.

He answered me on the first ring, I could hear the noises from Central in the background of the call, he was evidently in the office.

"Yes, I know, yes...the two policemen, how dead? I left them alive, bruised but alive!...where am I? I'm going to my house, I haven't slept for two nights. Okay! I come there, okay, for an interrogation? Why? They broke both of their necks, stunned by the explosion they didn't react. Okay! I repeat that they were ALIVE! Why didn't I call the ambulance right away? Why? I don't know ... I was in shock ... I saw they were alive and went to the car, started thinking about this case ... time flew by....where are they? I can't tell you, you'd have a patrol car pick me up. Commander, trust me, I'm a good detective...James was my friend, the girl, Eve Bloom I liked...yes...yes, okay I figured, better that way, I was in the hospital, I was forewarned about it....How suspended? Me suspended? Wait! Why? It stays on the service record! No! I don't deserve it!" I hung up the communication.

Suspended--dead Vermont and Louis, their necks broken.

Game over for Eve, a pang in my heart made me remember her beautiful face.

"I'm sorry...I am Love....now rest, you are tired..." an angelic voice blew in my ear. I could feel her presence, I knew the child was there. She may not have been able to spread her wings, but she was there, for me. She was Love.

I was in pain, though.

I was sad and discouraged.

I ordered a long, hot, black coffee.

Queens was swarming with operations, the young lady at the bistro smiled graciously at me, a kind brunette with soft features and big dark eyes.

I smiled at her too, feeling crushed by the sheer volume of nefarious events. They were really all dead. Could it be that it was only one murderer? So well organized? Perhaps an ex-military man, an enthusiast of weapons, detonators, offensive fighting, a strategist who did not fear law enforcement. Perhaps he knew how they moved. But why?

The little girl with blond braids stroked the back of my neck gently.

"I Am Love."

Motive was really key to understanding where to go fishing for this individual. Or these individuals.

The coffee at first sip gave me a slight heartburn, the hot liquid however galvanized me.

I closed my eyes, I found myself cooped up in the reliable Dodge on the side of the road in front of the Korean restaurant.

"Sleep Adam...I am Love."

It was early, I could rest.

No one knew of this information, James was the only one along with Eve, but they were dead.

I had not yet verbalized.

So I would have no interruptions, or uncomfortable partners.

I dozed off.

Eve's face accompanied me.

I followed her gaze; I knew I was asleep but the dream was so lucid and true that I doubted it.

REM dream space

Date: December 25, 2023

Time: 4:45 PM

Eve pointed with her index finger to a door to open, her finger was diaphanous and graceful with long nails enameled carmine red.

I stared at the door, made of wood, inscribed with a famous Latin phrase "Per aspera ad astra" in cursive gold letters.

The iron knocker was heavy, I pushed it and the door gave way without resistance.

It was a church, a seemingly empty church with barrel vaults and arches held up by Doric columns. In the center of the nave flowers surrounded a covered coffin.

I walked through the series of horizontally arranged pews, down the central aisle. The marble beneath my feet produced an uneasy sound under my Nikes.

Eve followed me, I could hear her footsteps behind mine.

I stared at the coffin, I had to open it, I knew it, I didn't want to, I really didn't want to, and yet...Eve pointed to the coffin.

I uncovered it.

Inside was me.

Dead, dressed in a fancy suit, beard trimmed, hair combed.

I looked at her.

"What do you mean?"

I let the coffin close and gripped her shoulders tightly.

"Turn around," she whispered.

I turned around, letting go of her shoulders.

The church was packed; in the pews, on each pew, five people were sitting diligently.

I looked at them. They were me.

They were everyone, me.

"What's going on? What do you want to tell me?"

"You know!"

She vanished, the Church vanished, my many me's vanished.

I was in the Dodge, a dusky light entered the cockpit, the swarming of the street, the honking of cabs, two children playing ball in the distance brought me into the present moment.

Two people were entering the Korean club in front of me.

I straightened up; the dream was forgotten.

I got out of the Dodge and crossed the street.

CHAPTER SEVEN

Milky Way foreground, Queens.

Date: Dec. 25, 2023

Time: 5:54 PM

Adam carefully observed the faces inside the restaurant.

Anonymous faces, seated at an oval table, set with plastic placemats and shoddy plates.

He sat down, deciding to tergiver for the moment, waiting for everyone to take their seats.

At the entrance, two figures, like columns, watched us. I knew who they were.

They had accompanied us up to that moment.

The angelic child with wings enclosed diligently on the left, and the smelly boar with red eyes and shaggy gray fur, on the right.

They were part of the tragedy. They were the tragedy.

At the apex of the oval, a man with a prominent belly crushed by permissive buttons and at their most restrained, still standing stared at the diners who sat slowly but diligently. Some greeted with pats on the back, while others absorbed in their own thoughts searched the table for his name. They were assigned seats. I looked at my marker. It was white. The thirteenth seat, evidently.

"Well my dears! I see you have all arrived on time, and I am pleased to wish you all a very merry Christmas and an equally merry start! This operation will bring us the bliss we had been longing for, and now that we are at the finish line, I am glad that my friends, my fellow soldiers, those who began this adventure with me, are taking their seats!" the fat man spoke, twirling his hands emphatically; it would have appeared exaggerated if his tailored suit and the deferential air of the others, made one imagine that he was more than a sweaty host.

I stared at the others in their faces, gray, or bald, or bearded. No women. Only men 45 to 65 years old, Caucasian, well-to-do.

"You disciples of Noetike Synaxis know my name, but I repeat it for everyone, I am Theodore Alphonse. I lead this group from the beginning. And it was an important beginning, unaware we wondered if the promises would be kept, if our one guide would keep the agreements." Pause, overview of listeners.

"Here may I ask you to go into your wallet and look at the balance?"

Each of those present took pains to pull out their phones; after a few transactions, I noticed satisfied looks as they placed the various devices back into their jacket pockets.

"As you have noticed, the promises have been kept. The bitcoins were transferred from the Ledger wallet, the master granted consent and authorized that they be withdrawn and deposited into your accounts.

The transaction on the dark web was smooth and easy, on Athos78 we replenished through the Dark Market, on Botmans World we purchased several thousand dollars worth of ammunition. But what until recently seemed incredibly unattainable, on the Killing forums it was easy to order attacks, not cheap, but on par with a hotel reservation.

Targets didn't stand a chance, a double attack was agreed upon, in case they escaped the first one and two goons for each victim.

All, I repeat all, my disciples, all targets have been eliminated.

And as a result, the well-known and definite commission rewards us for the expenses incurred to date."

A round of applause interrupted him.

The applause waned that one of them stood up and took the floor:

"I am James The Zebedee, you know I was skeptical, in fact I had to change my mind, now I stand before you for the last act of our play. I know that among us, there is HE, I ask that he will come forth and explain to us why he has requested our services. Thank you, I know he will." and he sat back down.

"I don't think HE will want to talk to us. But I thank you for soliciting him. I confirm that HE is here with us."

A burly bearded man with a deep European accent intervened.

"I am Simon Canaanite, I passed the proxies for you to access the Dark Web with different firewalls, our conversations were encrypted and protected, no one can trace them back to us. The sites themselves protected our identities, the transactions were done in cryptocurrency through wallets that ensured anonymity with eight-digit encryption codes and most importantly absolute security in authorizing the transaction. So now we could get up with our already deposited wealth and get the hell out of here. This would carry no penalty, I would like to point out, because the last act for some might be onerous. Better we all be sure of what we are doing."

"I agree Simon and I thank you for that as usual you are efficient and incontrovertible."

Silence fell over us.

A pudgy, sweaty man, forced into a cashmere turtleneck sweater, stood up.

"I am Bartholomew, I have business all over the world, two grown-up daughters, two divorces, and a few mistresses who want me for my money and from whom I must obviously defend myself. I can't stay. Really, I have been fine with you, but I want to continue my business otherwise. Because of the oath I took, I will keep to our pact, not revealing names and courses of action but I would really like to take up Simone's proposal." he stared hopefully at the coven leader.

"Go, you have been given the chance now. Those who wish to follow it should do so now, otherwise we will proceed with the evening."

Bartholomew hurried away. His haste intimidated me. The others stared into the void or at distant spots where they could take refuge.

The sound of the door closing opened the last act. A rustle of wings as a flock of doves rose into the air, filled my auricle.

"Get up and thank us," the lackey demanded, allowing no room for replies.

"Get up, grrrr, my soul," I complied.

"Who are you?" Theodore asked with grandiose importance. I automatically replied,

"I am HIM."

The truth unfolded before my eyes, like inside a coffin, in my coffin, with Eve's face next to mine.

"WE KNOW," all twelve diners chorused. Silence fell in the room. Many eyes fixed on me.

"Before we proceed, do you want to explain why you contacted us? Now you can truly feel free; we are at the end."

"I wanted to advance in my career... the Commander had prevented me until now because he believed I had no merit... some bureaucratic loophole, and I was a Detective for too long..."

"We know that's not the real reason, right Adam?" Theodore pressed. "I wanted to know what it feels like. I've been on the side of right, of the Law for too long. Balance corrupted me." I put my hands in my hair. A growl made me feel at home. Balance. "Now you tell the truth." All twelve participants chorused,

"THANK YOU!"

"What happens now?" Theodore gestured to pour the wine into each flute. The boar with its heavy hooves approached each diner, distributing the red liquid in glasses. The rhythmic stamping intoxicated me with anticipation. I saw drool dripping from its fierce jaw, its coarse hair curving on its back to reach the mighty coriaceous horns.

"Now, let's toast."

I stared at my glass, which remained empty. "Not you. Everything is organized. The evidence against us will be spread on the web shortly. Now go out, we don't want you to watch, but THANK YOU for using our services!"

"What happens? What have I commissioned? I want to know; I don't remember; I'm stunned! Theodore, tell me!"

"I know, I know, relax, breathe; everything is perfect, everything is happening as you requested. In ten minutes, your department's police will enter the place; you will explain that you followed us and show what you did."

"What have I done?" I was alarmed.

"Let's drink, brothers! There's no more time! And THANK YOU!"

All of them raised their glasses and drank the red liquid in the flutes. "Get out, HIM; wait for your teammates; glory has come from you! Perhaps a medal awaits you! Now go!" Theodore proclaimed with emphasis. I headed towards the exit, not understanding what I would say to the team that would arrive shortly; I already heard the sirens in the distance. Theodore contorted, closing in on his abdomen; he emitted a choked guttural sound and fell to the ground, white foam coming out of his mouth.

One after the other, the lackeys collapsed on the table or on the floor, frothing and writhing, squirming like soft worms on a viscous and damp terrain.

Smell of urine and vomit, blood, and viscera that extricated from mature bodies. Screams and sobs that, in the Hades of that dirty linoleum floor, entwined souls at that last moment of vital breath.

Next to me, near the exit door, the last man vomited blood, then, looking at the sky, he fell dramatically to his knees at my feet, with his eye sockets turned towards the sky in prayer. His body collapsed entirely with all his weight finally aware of gravity, on the gray plastic tiles.

Tunc.

I turned around.

They were dead.

All dead. Poisoned by the wine.

Deliberately.

I had orchestrated everything.

In my hand, I held the final stanza.

"In a realm of darkness, Adam advances,

Twelve friends, justice in balance.

With words of gold and hearts of light,

Silent victors, evil they guide.

Day and night, their commitment grows,

Twelve shadows, goodness bestows.

In a world where injustice seeks its place,

Adam and friends vanish in their embrace."

I curled up, it was no longer necessary.

Would they believe me?

Were there traces of my transactions in the Dark Web?

"Of course not, grrrr," replied the usual voice.

The police car stopped in front of me.

The Commander stepped out, a black man with pectorals like shields and a well-camouflaged gray baldness.

"Detective! Your call put us on alert! What does it mean, handing over the entire gang?"

"They're inside, dead, Commander..." I reported, strangely and cowardly.

"Dead? Did you kill them?"

"No, poisoned. Maybe one of them betrayed them, but they played the Christmas Game, the rhymes, the various deaths, it was all their doing."

"How did you figure it out? Come in, armed and vigilant!"

I sat in the car. I was tired.

Eve, I'm sorry for sacrificing you, you were so beautiful.

"Why did they plan all these murders, and how did you figure it out?"

"The last rhyme, Eve Bloom helped us decipher it and brought us here. The victims were part of a game, a Game, you understand? It's used on the Web; someone had to find them. The Game also includes this, the solution."

"Game, Web, what are you saying? There will be an investigation, you know?"

"Yes, it will come out that I'm a hero. I found them, and I was present at their end to warn you. Look into their files, the transactions they made, find the killers they confirmed, and it will come out that I discovered everything. Maybe they would have continued, maybe not. But the case is closed, Commander. You'll understand everything from my report."

He looked at me surprised.

An officer rushed to report, "Commander, twelve men poisoned, presumably. I'm calling the forensics team and collecting evidence."

The Commander looked at me, and I delivered my final line, scratching my overly long beard:

"And I shut it down!"

A LIFE OF STARS LIBRARY®

VAT number 03624001206

Viktor A. King: A Master of International Horror

Known globally for his extraordinary ability to weave compelling and terrifying stories, Viktor A. King stands out as one of the prominent authors in the world of horror. With nine publications under his belt, his talent has been translated into six different languages, bringing his dark literary genius to readers around the globe.

Born in the obscure atmosphere of winter nights, Viktor A. King has always shown an affinity for the darker side of life. His writing evokes palpable tension, transporting readers into worlds where horror and mystery intertwine in an unsettling embrace.

Among his most celebrated works, titles like "Stay Woke" and "Veil of Shadows" emerge as pieces that have frightened and fascinated millions of readers. Each of his works is a journey into the unknown, where spectral creatures and dark secrets unfold page by page.

His latest novel, "Diamonds Bloke," is a milestone in his career, promising to immerse the reader in a world of obscene intrigues and unspeakable horrors. With prose as sharp as a knife and a captivating plot, King continues to solidify his reputation as a master of contemporary horror.

Thanks to his ability to transform humanity's deepest fears into engaging tales, Viktor A. King has earned a prominent place in modern horror literature. With each new publication, he continues to demonstrate his mastery in the art of chilling and enchanting readers from every corner of the planet. Prepare to delve into darkness with Viktor A. King, where every page is a step into the unknown.

Dear readers,

It is with immense gratitude and a heart full of emotions that I address you today. I write this letter filled with appreciation as I reflect on the incredible journey we have shared through the pages of my books.

I would like to express my sincere gratitude to each of you who has embraced the darkness and ventured into the dark worlds I have created. Your support and admiration are the cornerstone of my inspiration, and every word I have written has been shaped by your constant presence.

The success of every book is a miracle made possible by your passion for horror and compelling storytelling. Reading your reviews, hearing your stories about the emotions you felt as you traversed the pages, I realize how closely bound we are in this literary journey.

"Diamonds Bloke," my latest novel, was a special project for me, and seeing your reaction has been the best gift I could receive. Every single comment, every share, has been a light in the dark night of creation, and I am eternally grateful for every kind word you've spent on it.

Your affection has driven me to explore new horizons of horror, to try to bring you experiences that keep you awake at night and make you reflect in the quiet moments. You are my source of inspiration, and your passion fuels the fire of my creativity.

Thank you, again, for being part of this journey. You are the reason I continue to write, dream, and venture into the uncharted lands of dark narrative. I look forward to sharing with you new adventures and thrills in the upcoming chapters of our shared story.

With deep gratitude,

Viktor A. King

By the Same Author

Game of Genetic Anomalies

Liquid Balance

Phantom's Silent Oath

Tacit Resonances

Black Red Blood White

Veil of Shadows

Stay Woke

Diamonds Blake

Translated into Six Languages

A LIFE OF STARS LIBRARY®

VAT number 03624001206

COPYRIGHT © VIKTOR A. KING ©

"In the ink of the unknown, terror whispers.

Brace yourself what lurks in shadows is but a glimpse of the unspeakable horrors ahead."

Viktor A. King